I CAN'T GET MY TURTLE TO MOVE

I CAN'T GET MY TURTLE TO MOVE

Elizabeth Lee O'Donnell
Pictures by Maxie Chambliss

HOUGHTON MIFFLIN COMPANY BOSTON

Atlanta   Dallas   Geneva, Illinois   Palo Alto   Princeton   Toronto

1995 Impression
Houghton Mifflin Edition, 1993

Printed in the U.S.A.
ISBN: 0-395-61752-9
23456789-FL-96 95 94

For Marta

One turtle sleeping in the sun.

"Walk!" I say.

"Blink," I say.

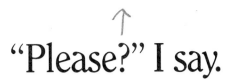

"Please?" I say.

But I can't get my turtle to move.

Two goldfish hiding in the weeds.
"Swim," I say, and they do.

But I can't get my turtle to move.

Three kittens tangling up the yarn.
"Purr," I say, and they do.

But I can't get my turtle to move.

14

Four puppies napping in the barn.
"Sit," I say, and they do.

But I can't get my turtle to move.

Five butterflies threading in and out.
"Sip," I say, and they do.

But I can't get my turtle to move.

Six inchworms hiking up a leaf.
"Munch," I say, and they do.

But I can't get my turtle to move.

Seven ants talking nose to nose.
"March," I say, and they do.

But I can't get my turtle to move.

Eight hens clucking on the fence.
"Peck," I say, and they do.

But I can't get my turtle to move.

Nine crows eating up the corn.
"Shoo," I say, and they do.

But I can't get my turtle to move.

Ten rabbits nibbling lettuce leaves.
"Hop," I say, and they do.

But I can't get my turtle to move.

One turtle sleeping in the sun.
"Hey!" I say. "Guess what?" I say. "Lunch!" I say.

I get my turtle to move!